My Emotions Through Emojis

FEELING HAPPY

BY
THEIA LAKE

Enslow
PUBLISHING

Please visit our website, www.enslow.com.
For a free color catalog of all our high-quality books, call toll free 1-800-398-2504 or fax 1-877-980-4454.

Library of Congress Cataloging-in-Publication Data
Names: Lake, Theia, author.
Title: Feeling happy / Theia Lake.
Description: Buffalo, New York : Enslow Publishing, [2024] | Series: My emotions through emojis | Includes index.
Identifiers: LCCN 2022056217 (print) | LCCN 2022056218 (ebook) | ISBN 9781978533431 (library binding) | ISBN 9781978533424 (paperback) | ISBN 9781978533448 (ebook)
Subjects: LCSH: Happiness–Juvenile literature. | Emotions in children–Juvenile literature.
Classification: LCC BF575.H27 L35 2023 (print) | LCC BF575.H27 (ebook) | DDC 155.4/1242–dc23/eng/20221121
LC record available at https://lccn.loc.gov/2022056217
LC ebook record available at https://lccn.loc.gov/2022056218

Published in 2024 by
Enslow Publishing
2544 Clinton Street
Buffalo, NY 14224

Designer: Tanya Dellaccio Keeney
Editor: Theresa Emminizer

Photo credits: Cover (phone) Victor Z/Shutterstock.com; cover, series art (clouds) Theus/Shutterstock.com; cover, series art (emojis) stas11/Shutterstock.com; pp. 5, 9 Roman Samborskyi/Shutterstock.com; p. 7 Pavel Kobysh/Shutterstock.com; p. 11 Pixel-Shot/Shutterstock.com; p. 13 Ground Picture/Shutterstock.com; p. 15 EpicStockMedia/Shuttertock.com; p. 17 Pressmaster/Shutterstock.com; p. 19 kryzhov/Shutterstock.com; p. 21 Monkey Business Images/Shutterstock.com.

Printed in the United States of America

CPSIA compliance information: Batch #CS24ENS: For further information contact Enslow Publishing, at 1-800-398-2504.

CONTENTS

Boldface words appear in Words to Know.

ARE YOU HAPPY?

We all have lots of different feelings inside us. Sometimes we're sad. Sometimes we're mad. Sometimes we're happy! Happiness is one of the best feelings. When you're happy, you feel bright. You feel lively. You feel full of joy!

WHAT A GOOD FEELING!

Asher loves to ride his bike 😃! He loves to feel the wind on his face. He loves to **pedal** fast and fly through the park! When he's riding his bike, Asher doesn't think about anything else 😎. He's so happy 😊!

WHAT MAKES YOU HAPPY?

Is there an **activity** that always puts a smile on your face? Maybe you love to dance and sing! Maybe you like to paint. Everybody is different. That's why we all have different things that make us happy!

HOW DIFFERENT!

Serena is playing at her friend Charlie's house. Charlie likes **puzzles** 😊. Serena would rather draw! But she likes seeing Charlie happy. It makes her happy too 🤗! Charlie and Serena put together a puzzle. Then they draw pictures together 😁.

HAPPY PEOPLE

Sometimes it's not an activity that makes us happy, it's a person! When you're with someone you love, you feel safe. You feel good. You feel happy! Can you think of someone that makes you happy?

BEST FRIENDS

Teddy, Simon, and Clark are best friends. They do everything together! When Simon is sad 🙁, it helps to tell Teddy and Clark. When he's **excited** 😁 about something, they're the first people he talks to! Being friends makes the boys very happy 😌😌😌.

HAPPY PLACES

Sometimes being in a certain place makes us happy. Maybe it's the home of someone you love. Maybe it's a place where you always have fun, like the soccer field or the playground. Can you think of a place where you feel happy?

A SPECIAL SPOT

Kit has five brothers and sisters 😳. She loves them very much, but sometimes she likes time by herself 😊! Kit has a special spot to go. It's a **fort**! She made it herself 🤗. Kit always feels happy in her fort 😁.

GET HAPPY!

When do you feel happy? Is it when you're doing something you love? Is it when you're with your **favorite** people? Is it when you're in a special place? Maybe it's all three! There are many wonderful ways to feel happy.

WORDS TO KNOW

activity: Something to do.

excited: Feeling lively or happy about something.

favorite: Something you love best.

fort: A tent or shelter made by hand.

pedal: To push the foot holds on a bike to make it move. Also the name of the foot holds.

puzzle: A game or toy to put together piece by piece.

FOR MORE INFORMATION

BOOKS

Falcón Maldonado, Cristina. *I'm Happy to Be Me!* New York, NY: Windmill Books, 2020.

Wood, John. *Harry the Hamster Feels Happy*. New York, NY: Windmill Books, 2020.

WEBSITES

British Council
learnenglishkids.britishcouncil.org/songs/feelings-are-feelings
Listen to songs and play games about feelings.

Kids Health
kidshealth.org/en/kids/talk-feelings.html
Learn how to name and talk about your feelings.

Publisher's note to educators and parents: Our editors have carefully reviewed these websites to ensure that they are suitable for students. Many websites change frequently, however, and we cannot guarantee that a site's future contents will continue to meet our high standards of quality and educational value. Be advised that students should be closely supervised whenever they access the internet.

INDEX